Frank and the Bad Surprise

Martha Brockenbrough

illustrated by Jon Lau

LQ
LEVINE QUERIDO

MONTCLAIR · AMSTERDAM · HOBOKEN

This is an Arthur A. Levine book
Published by Levine Querido

LQ

LEVINE QUERIDO

www.levinequerido.com • info@levinequerido.com
Levine Querido is distributed by Chronicle Books, LLC
Text copyright © 2022 by Martha Brockenbrough
Illustrations copyright © 2022 by Jon Lau
All rights reserved
Library of Congress Cataloging-in-Publication data is available
ISBN 978-1-64614-088-6
Printed and bound in China

```
        TM
  [FSC logo]      MIX
                  Paper from
                  responsible sources
  FSC
  www.fsc.org     FSC™ C104723
```

Published in April 2022
First Printing
The text type was set in Perpetua Regular
Jon Lau created the illustrations for
this picture book by painting the characters, objects,
and backgrounds using poster color paints on sheets
of BFK Rives printmaking paper.
He then scanned the paintings and assembled the illustrations
in Adobe Photoshop, much like a digital collage.

To Ann, Tracy, Junyi, Nikko, Ben, Sam, and Dad
— *J. L.*

To Lucy and Alice
— *M. B.*

CHAPTER 1

The Bad Surprise

Frank the cat had it good.

He had a nice house, lots of toys, all the Whiskies he could eat, and a window that looked out at the world.

Frank should have known this good life could not last. One day, he looked out his window.

He saw blue skies, swooping birds, and a person bringing mail. Frank loved all of these things.

Even better, Frank saw his humans.

Frank's humans parked their
car. They got out. They pulled a box
from the back.

"A box," Frank thought. "A box for me! There is no better present. I will climb inside and make it my lair."

But the box was not a present. It would not be his lair.

The box was bad news.

Frank knew what to do.

Frank typed a letter.

To my dear humans:

We do not need the puppy. We were happy with life the way it was before. It is time to take the puppy back.

Sincerely,

Frank

Frank folded the letter, tucked it
in an envelope, and put it in the mail.
Frank was pleased. The letter
would do the trick. The dog would go
away. Frank would have it good again.

It was hard work to make a good life. Frank found a sunbeam. He lay down. He closed his eyes. Maybe the puppy would be gone by the time he woke up.

That was a nice thought. Almost as nice as a sunbeam on a pillow.

CHAPTER 2

The Rules of Naps

There is nothing bad about a nap. A nap in a warm spot is cozy. A nap feels the way warm bread and butter taste.

Frank loved naps more than any other thing.

Frank's humans knew not to wake him from a nap.

They knew that was against the
rules of naps.

The puppy did not care about
the rules of naps.

Frank opened his eyes.

Frank rubbed his nose.

His nose was wet.

The puppy wagged her tail at Frank.

The puppy
blinked at Frank.
The puppy panted
her hot breath on Frank.

Frank did not like hot breath.
Frank swished his tail.

Frank swatted the puppy. It was
not a big swat. It was a small swat
and the puppy had it coming.

18

But this was
not how Frank's
humans saw it.

Luckily, Frank could still reach
his keyboard.

To my dear humans:

This is unfair. The puppy broke the rules of naps.

The puppy should be in jail, not me.

If you let me out and send the puppy away, I will forgive you.

Firmly,

Frank

Frank waited.

He waited until the sun went down and his belly growled for Whiskies.

Frank peered out. The puppy was eating his Whiskies.

Frank yowled.

CHAPTER 3

They Forgot about Frank

"Oh, Frank!" the humans said. "We forgot about you."

They let Frank out of jail. They had not even read Frank's letter.

Frank sat on his human's lap. Frank did not purr. His human stroked Frank's back. It felt good. But Frank still did not purr.

"Frank," the human said, "You must be nice to the puppy."

Frank slid off his human's lap.

Nice to the puppy? The puppy who broke the rules of naps and licked and had hot breath and stole Frank's Whiskies? *Please.*

Frank wrote another letter.

To my dear humans:

This is too much for any cat to handle. The time has come for me to find a new home.

Good luck with that puppy.

You will need it.

Your former cat,

Frank

Frank put the letter by the door.

This time, his humans would be sure to see it. They would know what they had done. They would know why he had to run away. They would feel bad, all the way to their bones.

And if the puppy licked them, well, they would deserve it.

The humans would miss Frank. They would miss his plush fur.

They would miss
his purrs.

They would miss
the tricks he did
with feathers on sticks and balls
with bells.

But there was nothing to be done.

They had put Frank in jail. They had been unfair. They had brought a puppy into the house, and now they would have to live without Frank.

Frank was not the sort to shed a tear, but he did feel sorry for his humans. It would be a big loss for them.

The next day, the humans took the puppy outside to pee. The puppy was too dumb to know how to pee in litter like Frank did. Frank slipped out the open door.

"Goodbye, old life," Frank said.

It was a shame he could not take anything with him. Not his feather on a stick.

Not his ball with a bell.

Not even his keyboard.

The puppy had wrecked everything.

This was not fair. But it was the way of the world. Just when you think you've got it good, someone brings home a puppy.

Frank shook his head.

Then he set off.

CHAPTER 4

Frank Runs Away

Frank had spent a lot of time looking out his window at the world, so he knew what was what.

He knew where the dogs lived. He would not go there. He did not need their tongues and teeth and tails.

Frank knew where the cats lived. He would not go there either. He did not want to live with other cats. That would mean sharing things. No thanks.

It was strange to be on the far side of the window. It was not the

same out there. It was noisier.
The sidewalk was not as smooth as
it had looked. The cars went by so
fast. They splashed Frank with
puddles.

Frank was wet all over. "That
puppy," he thought. "I blame her."

Frank went to a house that had no cats or dogs.

They will let me in, he thought. They will say, "Welcome, Frank. We always wanted a cat. Here is your new sofa. Here is your new sunbeam. Here is your new feather on a stick. We do not have a ball with a bell, but we will buy you one."

Frank would sit on their laps. He would purr.

It would not be the exact same life he had.

But it could be a good life, all the
same. Frank meowed.

Then he waited for his new life
to start.

CHAPTER 5

Shoo

After a bit, a man came to the door.

He wore a robe and held a cup of coffee. He rubbed his eyes and looked down.

"You," the man said. "You woke me up."

"Meow," Frank said.

"Shoo," the man said. "Scat!"

He scooted Frank away with his

foot. It did not hurt, but it was not

okay. Frank would not live with such a brute. No way.

The house next door had flowers, and the flowers had bees and butterflies. Frank swished his tail. He would like to look at them, but looking was better from indoors.

He sat on the porch.

"Meow?" he said.

The door opened. A ball of fur with lots of teeth burst out. It barked like mad and Frank was sorry he had ever said meow on that porch.

He had not seen the dog from
his old window. No wonder, though.
When you have a dog that bad, you
do not show it off.

"That dog is a mess," Frank said.

"That is what happens when you get

a puppy."

Frank stood on the sidewalk.

"Things could not get worse,"
Frank said.

Then it started to rain.

CHAPTER 6

Things Can Always Get Worse

The rain felt like the tongues of many puppies.

Frank slunk down the sidewalk. Each house looked warm and dry inside. The warmest and driest house of all was his.

Frank sat on the sidewalk in

front of his old home. Through his
old window, he could see the puppy.
The puppy was taking a nap.

A garbage truck passed. A sack
of trash popped out and burst.

It was gross trash: lint and fruit peels
and eggshells and tea bags.

Some got on Frank.

Frank was not only wet, Frank
also stank.

But Frank did not say, "Things couldn't get worse."

This is because Frank had learned that things can *always* get worse. Frank had learned a lesson.

"I do not like lessons," said Frank.

Lessons would be the sort of thing Frank would write angry letters about if Frank still could.

Frank would write a letter to the garbage company about yucky trash.

Frank would write a letter to grumpy men in robes.

To people with small dogs that yapped and chased.

Frank would also write a letter
to the sky. What good were clouds
and rain? He shook a paw and hissed.

And then the sky lit up and
boomed.

The boom rattled the window. The puppy's ears perked up. Puppy was awake.

"Ha," Frank thought. "Now you know how it feels when something wrecks your nap."

The puppy shook. The puppy looked scared.

"Ha," Frank said. But he didn't mean it.

No one, not even a puppy, should feel scared.

The puppy stood and looked out the window. She wagged her tail. Her small, pink tongue hung out of her mouth.

"Go ahead," Frank said. "Laugh at me."

CHAPTER 7

Frank Writes One Last Letter

The puppy did not laugh at Frank.

The puppy barked.

She barked and barked, and soon, Frank's humans came to the window.

They pointed at Frank and opened their mouths.

Then they opened the door.

"Frank," they said, "Come inside! We have missed you so!"

Frank blinked the rain out of his eyes.

Did he want to go inside?

Did he want to be with his humans, who had brought home a puppy?

The puppy who saved him from the rain?

Frank did.
Inside the
house, it was
warm and dry.

His bowl was now
up high, where he could reach his
Whiskies, but the puppy could not.

There were
laps for him to
sit on, laps
and hands
and towels to
dry him.

Best of all, there was also a
puppy who had nice warm breath
and plush fur of her own.

It turned out there was something better than a sunbeam on a
couch.

That night, after
everyone had gone to bed,
Frank started a new letter.

To my dear humans:

The puppy won't feel like this is her home too if you don't give her a name.

I have taken the liberty of giving her one myself.

Sincerely yours,

Frank

Then Frank wrote himself a
to-do list. He had so much to teach
Sunny about the world.

"I used to have it good, but I
don't have it good anymore," Frank
thought.

"But that is because I have it great."

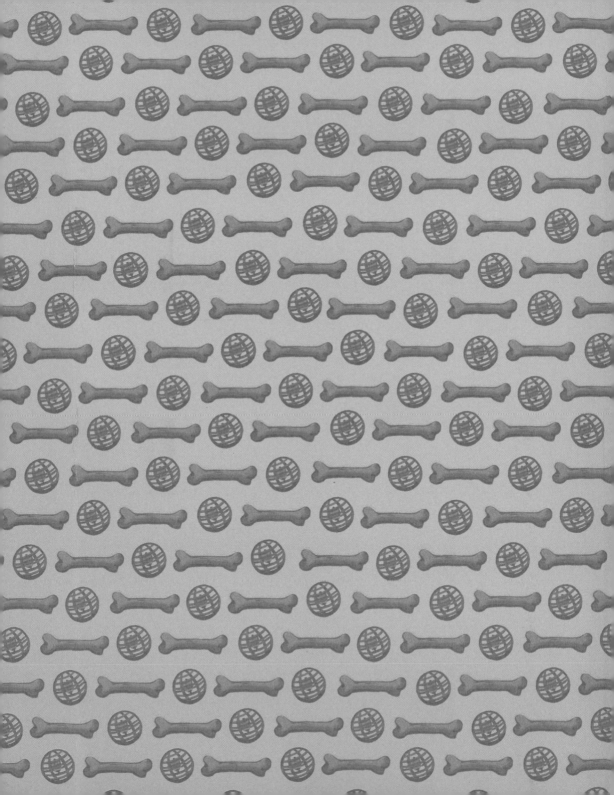